GERMAN SHEPHERDS

KATIE LAJINESS

Big Buddy Books
An Imprint of Abdo Publishing
abdopublishing.com

BIG BUDDY DOGS

abdopublishing.com

Published by Abdo Publishing, a division of ABDO, PO Box 398166, Minneapolis, Minnesota 55439.

Big Buddy Books™ is a trademark and logo of Abdo Publishing.

Printed in the United States of America, North Mankato, Minnesota.
092017
012018

THIS BOOK CONTAINS RECYCLED MATERIALS

Cover Photo: Getty Images.
Interior Photos: AP Photo/John Spink, AJC (p. 11); Drew Angerer/Getty Images (p. 5); Getty Images (pp. 7, 9, 13, 15, 17, 19, 21, 23, 25, 27, 29, 30).

Coordinating Series Editor: Tamara L. Britton
Contributing Editor: Jill Roesler
Graphic Design: Jenny Christensen

Publisher's Cataloging-in-Publication Data

Names: Lajiness, Katie, author.
Title: German shepherds / by Katie Lajiness.
Description: Minneapolis, Minnesota : Abdo Publishing, 2018. | Series: Big buddy dogs | Includes online resources and index.
Identifiers: LCCN 2017943933 | ISBN 9781532112096 (lib.bdg.) | ISBN 9781614799160 (ebook)
Subjects: LCSH: German shepherd dog--Juvenile literature. | Dogs--Juvenile literature.
Classification: DDC 636.73--dc23
LC record available at https://lccn.loc.gov/2017943933

CONTENTS

A POPULAR BREED

Dogs are popular pets. Today, Americans own more than 78 million! Around the world, there are more than 400 dog **breeds**.

One of these is the German shepherd. Let's learn why the German shepherd is the second-most popular breed in the United States.

A German shepherd won the Best in Show prize at the 2017 Westminster Kennel Club Dog Show.

THE DOG FAMILY

Dogs come in all shapes and sizes. Yet all dogs belong to the **Canidae** family. The name comes from the Latin word for dog, which is *canis*. This family includes coyotes, foxes, wolves, and more.

Humans and dogs have lived together for at least 16,000 years. In the beginning, humans **bred** them to hunt. Soon, they trained dogs to do other jobs such as guarding property and herding livestock.

Today, some German shepherds are trained to be guide dogs.

GERMAN SHEPHERDS

The German shepherd is a somewhat new **breed**. In the late 1800s, Captain Max von Stephanitz of Germany bred a shepherd dog with a wolf-mix dog. He wanted brave, hardworking dogs to protect and herd his sheep. He called them German shepherds.

German shepherds were once known as wolf dogs.

The **breed** spread from Germany to other countries. In 1908, the German shepherd joined the **American Kennel Club (AKC)**.

Beginning in the 1920s, trainers taught German shepherds to lead blind people. These were the first guide dogs. Today, German shepherds can be family pets or service dogs.

Did you know?

The AKC includes the German shepherd in the Herding Group. Herding dogs are able to control the movement of other animals.

German shepherds can be trained to search for people who are hurt.

WHAT THEY'RE LIKE

The German shepherd is a smart **breed** that loves to be with people. They can quickly learn new tricks. German shepherds are also loyal companions who love to play with their owners.

German shepherds used for the police and military often come from Europe. The shepherds bred in the United States are not as forceful.

COAT AND COLOR

German shepherds usually have black and tan fur. Most have a double coat. The outer coat is medium length and wiry. It **repels** water to keep the dog dry in all weather conditions. The undercoat is short and thick for warmth.

A German shepherd can also have a gray or red coat.

SIZE

German shepherds are strong, well-built dogs. They have long bodies for their height. These dogs have black noses, dark eyes, and ears that stand up.

The German shepherd is a tall dog. Males stand 24 to 26 inches (56 to 66 cm) tall. The females are somewhat smaller.

German shepherds weigh about 75 to 95 pounds (34 to 43 kg). The females weigh about 15 pounds (7 kg) less.

FEEDING

All dogs need food and water to supply energy. Quality dog food provides important **nutrients**. Dogs can eat moist, semimoist, and dry foods. Puppies eat three or more small meals a day. Adult dogs eat one to two times a day.

Every month, an adult German shepherd eats about 40 pounds (18 kg) of dry dog food.

CARE

Dogs require a lot of care. German shepherds need regular brushing to keep their coats healthy. Sometimes, they need a bath to help keep them clean. A dog should have its nails trimmed once a month. It should have its ears checked to avoid **infection**.

The German shepherd's bite has 238 pounds (108 kg) of force. A human's bite has just 120 pounds (54 kg) of force.

All dogs need a good veterinarian. The vet can provide health exams and **vaccines** for a German shepherd. He or she can also **spay** or **neuter** a dog.

Puppies will need to see the vet several times during their first few months. Adult dogs should visit the vet once a year for a checkup.

Like a human exam, a veterinarian will listen to a dog's heart and lungs with a stethoscope. The vet also looks at the eyes, ears, and nose, among other parts.

Every dog needs a collar with identification tags. A **microchip** can also keep a pet safe. This way, an owner can find a dog if it gets lost.

At home, a crate offers a German shepherd a place to rest. It can also help with housebreaking puppies.

Did you know?

Throughout their lifetime, one in three pets will get lost. Owners should make sure their pets always have a form of identification.

German shepherds have lots of energy. So, they need tough toys to chew on. If a shepherd gets bored, he might start chewing on the furniture!

PUPPIES

A German shepherd mother is **pregnant** for about 63 days. Then, she gives birth to a **litter** of six to nine puppies. Each newborn weighs about one pound (0.45 kg).

Shepherd puppies are born blind and deaf. Two weeks later, they can see and hear. At three weeks, the puppies take their first steps.

All German shepherds are born with floppy ears. At about seven to nine weeks old, their ears begin to stand up.

THINGS THEY NEED

At eight to 12 weeks old, German shepherd puppies are ready for **adoption**. When a puppy comes home, an owner should begin obedience training as soon as it is settled.

All puppies like to be active. So, they need daily exercise and training. A German shepherd will be a loving companion for ten to 12 years.

A German shepherd is the third most intelligent dog. Some say that border collies and poodles are smarter.

GLOSSARY

adoption the process of taking responsibility for a pet.

American Kennel Club (AKC) an organization that studies and promotes interest in purebred dogs.

breed a group of animals sharing the same appearance and features. To breed is to produce animals by mating.

Canidae (KAN-uh-dee) the scientific Latin name for the dog family. Members of this family are called canids. They include wolves, jackals, foxes, coyotes, and domestic dogs.

infection (ihn-FEHK-shuhn) the causing of an unhealthy condition by something harmful, such as bacteria.

litter all of the puppies born at one time to a mother dog.

microchip an electronic circuit placed under an animal's skin. A microchip contains identifying information that can be read by a scanner.

neuter (NOO-tuhr) to remove a male animal's reproductive glands.

nutrient (NOO-tree-uhnt) something found in food that living beings take in to live and grow.

pregnant having one or more babies growing within the body.

repel to push away.

spay to remove a female animal's reproductive organs.

vaccine (vak-SEEN) a shot given to prevent illness or disease.

ONLINE RESOURCES

Booklinks
NONFICTION NETWORK
FREE! ONLINE NONFICTION RESOURCES

To learn more about German shepherds, visit **abdobooklinks.com**. These links are routinely monitored and updated to provide the most current information available.

INDEX